NOT BORING!

My name is John Smith – the most boring name in the world. Dad says with a name like John Smith no one will EVER make fun of me. Mum says I'm "one in a MILLION". My sister says it makes me the most boring person in history. But do not judge a book by its cover. My life is ANYTHING but boring!

Scholastic Children's Books
An imprint of Scholastic Ltd
Euston House, 24 Eversholt Street
London, NW1 1DB, UK
Registered office: Westfield Road, Southam, Warwickshire, CV47 0RA
SCHOLASTIC and associated logos are trademarks and/or
registered trademarks of Scholastic Inc.

First published in the UK by Scholastic Ltd, 2015

ISBN 978 1407 15197 7

A CIP catalogue record for this book is available
from the British Library.

Printed by CPI Group (UK) Ltd, Croydon, CR0 4YY
Papers used by Scholastic Children's Books are made from
wood grown in sustainable forests.

1 3 5 7 9 10 8 6 4 2

www.scholastic.co.uk

To Lottie-Lou, Daisy-Doo ... and Florence too!

Chapter One

So I'm minding my own business, cramming liquorice gobstoppers into my mouth, when ...

"Wotcha?!"

... a great big lump of a fist smashes into my back.

"Well, well, if it's not Mr Nobody!" sneers Adam Virgo, World School Bully Champion.

Why does it always have to be me? It's not like I go round with a sign on my back

1

saying "Make my life a misery". (Actually I did once go round with a sign on my back saying "Make my life a misery", but I hadn't put it there.)

Well, it's time I stood up to Adam Virgo. I'm not letting this gorilla beast me in the playground. What I need is a smart reply, something he'll remember for ever.

So I blow a big massive raspberry right in his face.

BRBRBRBRBRBR!!!

After that Virgo decides it would be a really good idea to hang me upside down on the school gates with the words "I am John Smith. If you think I'm a no body, blow a raspberry in my face" in thick black marker down the front of my shirt.

"I'm not a nobody," I yell.

"Sorry," sneers Virgo, looking around, "did someone say something?"

I see my big sister and her bone-brained boyfriend sloping through the school gates. Hayley totally hates my guts and Rufus thinks I'm a complete non-starter. But still, family is family, they always stick by you.

"Hayley," I gurgle, "can you help me?"

Hayley looks at me and giggles.

"Nice work, Virgo," says Rufus.

They stare at the message on my shirt and both blow a raspberry.

The head teacher walks across the playground with a steaming mug of tea. He sees me hanging on the gates and reads the words. "'I am John Smith. If you think I'm a no body, blow a raspberry in my face. . .'

"This is disgraceful, absolutely disgraceful," he mutters darkly.

At last, someone to help me. Step aside, the cavalry is here!

"'Nobody' is spelled as one word!" says the head teacher. "Look it up in the dictionary – nobody: a person of no importance."

Everyone looks at me.

"Yes, head teacher," says Virgo. "I won't make that mistake again. . ."

"Too right you won't," barks the head teacher. "Give me that marker pen!" The head teacher snaps his fingers and Virgo hands him the thick black marker.

"Now pay close attention," says the head teacher. "It's nobody! Nobody! Nobody!"

He writes the words down three times on my shirt.

"John Smith is a nobody! Got that?" says the head teacher.

"John Smith is a nobody," says Virgo.

"John Smith is a nobody," says the head

teacher again. This time all the other teachers and most of the playground join in too.

"John Smith is a nobody!" they all cheer.

The head teacher looks me squarely in the eye. "You too, Smith, come on now. . ."

"John Smith is a nobody," I murmur.

"Excellent," says the head teacher. Then he blows a raspberry.

Then EVERYONE starts blowing raspberries. The other mums and dads, my fellow pupils ... even Mrs Williams, the lollipop lady!

Then they wander off, leaving me upside down on the school gate, alone with my tormentor. Virgo leans in really close. I can feel my heart thumping, the sweat running down the back of my neck, the liquorice gobstoppers gently rolling out of my pocket.

"I'm not finished with you, John Smith,"

sneers Virgo. "It's school sports day tomorrow and you know what that means?"

"We'll pair up on the same team, steer our side to victory and afterwards become best friends?" I nod hopefully.

"Almost," he chuckles. "It means I'm going to trample you into the mud."

He pops a gobstopper in his mouth and lumbers across the playground, chuckling.

Chapter Two

"You have to stand up to the bullies," whispers Granddad through a corridor of cereal cartons the next morning at the kitchen table.

Granddad lives with me and Mum and Dad and my big sister, Hayley, or as I like to call her, "mankind's greatest threat!"

We live in a normal little house on a normal little street in a normal little town with people and cars and offices, and under a sky that's sometimes blue but mostly grey. You probably have something like it yourself.

Hayley is sitting at the kitchen table doing her make-up. She's going to a party this afternoon and needs at least ten thousand hours in front of a mirror to make herself

look like a normal human being.

"Did I ever tell you about the time I was nearly eaten by a twenty-foot ballet dancer?" says Granddad.

Hayley rolls her eyes.

"Or when I danced with a live alligator?" he continues.

"Can't say you have, Granddad," I smile.

"I've been in some tight spots in my time," he nods. "But was I afraid? No, I certainly was not."

Hayley mouths the words with him, like she's heard it all a thousand times already. She thinks he's making it up. Only I know that Granddad is telling the truth. He really has had all these adventures.

Because Granddad belongs to something called the John Smith Club – which means if you're called John Smith, you can magically travel to other places and get into all kinds of scrapes. Since I joined the John Smith Club I've flown rockets through deepest, creepiest space and fought ferocious fiends like wild-eyed pirates and axe-wielding knights in armour! It's been such a brilliant adventure. But back in this world everyone thinks I'm just boring old John Smith; they have no idea what a hero – correction – superhero I really am.

Granddad puts his arm round my shoulder. "If you want to learn how to stand up for yourself, you've got to go to the place where men are men and sheep are sheep."

"Where's that, Granddad?" I shrug.

"Wales," says Hayley.

"I'm talking about the Wild West," says Granddad. "Where the real cowboys live! They'll teach you how to look after number one. Think you're up to it, son?"

"You try holding me back," I chortle.

Dad pokes his head out from under the

kitchen sink. "Talking of the Wild West, we had a couple of cowboys in here yesterday."

Wow! This is exciting stuff. Real-life cowboys in my house!

"What did they look like?" I gasp. "Did they have big hats and belts with lots of bullets? Were they called Ike or Doc or Wyatt?"

"I think one of them was called Dave," says Dad. "He had a big belly and a tattoo with his name on it in case he forgot what it was." Dad slides out from under the kitchen sink and gets to his feet. "They said they were plumbers. A complete pack of lies, of course."

Dad rummages in his toolbox and pulls out a spanner.

"Here you go," he says proudly, "the kitchen sink drama is almost over. I just need to tighten up the tap and we can all get on with our day…"

Granddad reaches towards the kitchen

sink. "I'll check the cold water's running..."

"NOT YET!" shouts Dad.

Granddad twists the cold tap and a jet of water shoots across the room, sploshing Hayley clean in the chops!

"It's a bullseye!" I chuckle.

Hayley's make-up runs down her face. She looks like a drowned panda! The only party she'll be going to is a tea party at the zoo.

"Oopsy..." says Granddad.

"Hello, Chin Chin, would you like some bamboo?" I laugh.

"You're such a child," snarls Hayley.

"That's because I'm eight," I giggle.

Granddad looks at me and winks. "My room in five minutes."

"But I've got school in half an hour," I protest.

"A man's gotta do what a man's gotta do..." he grins.

Chapter Three

"Right," puffs Granddad, "are you ready to go to the Wild West?"

He drags a battered old trunk out from underneath the bed. "Think you're up to the challenge?"

"I love a challenge, Granddad," I smile.

"That's my boy," he chuckles. "If I know one thing, it's this: the Wild West will make a man of you."

I like the sound of the Wild West. I want

to learn how to buck a bronco, how to win a duel, how to herd cattle... I want to be the greatest cowboy of all time.

Granddad reaches inside the trunk and brings out a cowboy hat and waistcoat. "Try this on for size."

I slip on my cowboy hat.

Granddad looks at me and smiles. "It fits you like a dream," he chuckles.

"Granddad, why is there a hole in the middle of the hat?" I mumble.

"That's a bullet hole from El Bandido the horse thief," mutters Granddad. "He pinched my ass when I wasn't looking. I was fuming!"

"I bet you were," I giggle.

"Stick your hand in your waistcoat, son," says Granddad. "Tell me what you find..."

I reach into the pocket and pull out a large silver coin.

"Wow," I gulp, "what's this, Granddad?"

"That," says Granddad, "is an American silver dollar. It's supposed to bring you good luck. Look after it — where you're going, you'll need it."

"I will, Granddad," I beam.

"OK, cowboy," he chuckles. "It's time to say the magic words."

I take a deep breath and say the words that will take me on my adventure.

"*Say it long, say it loud – I'm John Smith and I'm proud!*"

I hear horses' hooves pounding into the ground, the crack of a whip and the ping of bullets.

"Sounds pretty wild, Granddad!" I yell.

"I know," he replies. "I wish I was coming with you!"

Chapter Four

"Yeeeeeeeeee-haaaaaaaaaaaw!!!"

I'm bouncing round in the saddle as my horse gallops flat out across the desert. The steep orange walls of the canyon rise to a clear blue sky dotted with pillowy, puffy white clouds. Tumbleweed blows across the scrub and cactus plants prick the landscape.

Is being a cowboy just about the best thing ever? I say "yeehaw!" to that.

"Yeeeeeeeeee-haaaaaaaaaaaw!!!"

The horse finds a lick of pace. I lean forward and give it a big pat on the side of the neck.

Hold on a minute – this horse looks familiar, with its straggly mane of long brown hair and soft white diamond on the bridge of its nose. It's then I realize it's the same mad mare I had when I was a knight in armour!

"DAISY!!!"

Daisy snorts and nods, digs her hooves in the soil and puts on an extra burst of speed.

"N-O-o-O-o-O-o-O-o-O-o-O-o-O-o-O-o..."

I grip the reins and charge across the desert until I get to a one-horse, flyblown town. This is real cowboy stuff – the sun on my back, my shadow all long and thin on the ground and a little old man playing a mouth organ leaning against a wooden stump.

The houses up and down the street are made of timber, and they've got little porches at the front with rocking chairs. There's a hardware store too, and a barbershop, a local blacksmith and even a jailhouse, probably with a sheriff with his feet kicked up on his desk, his hat pulled over his eyes, taking an afternoon snooze.

I slow my horse to a lazy dawdle and stop outside a big house halfway up the street. Inside I hear the tinkling of a piano. I know what this place is; I've seen it in the movies Dad falls asleep to on a Sunday afternoon. This must be the saloon, where the real cowboy tough nuts hang out. Well, I'm going to show them that there is no grittier, meaner, tougher nut in the whole Wild West than John Smith!

I swing my legs out from the saddle and jump into a steaming pyramid of horse poo.

I look up and see a sign swinging on the breeze.

Welcome to Dungville, the pooiest
place in the West!

They're not joking. This place is a gut-wrenching, nostril-bending brew of horse doo-doo.

Suddenly the saloon doors fly open and a barefoot boy bundles out, clutching a little cloth cap in his hands. "Follow me, mister! There's a big fight going down."

A big fight in the saloon? Bring on the adventure!

I hitch up my trousers, squelch through the horse poo and kick open the saloon doors. They bounce straight back and knock me off my feet.

The boy lifts me up and dusts me down.

25

"Are you all right, sir?" says the barefoot boy.

"Oh, sure," I reply. "I was just horsing around."

We dive through the doors together. I want a piece of the action.

Inside, the saloon is a great big stew of arms and legs. Cowboys roll round in the sawdust wrestling each other, crashing into tables, swinging on chandeliers. There isn't a single person who isn't brawling with someone else. Even the little old lady sitting on the bar is cracking heads with her fancy umbrella. And everyone has a big bushy moustache – including the little old lady. All the while someone is hammering out a merry tune on a piano.

I turn to the barefoot boy in rags and shout in his ear. "Do they always fight like this?"

"No way," says the barefoot boy. "Most

days it's much worse! By the way, you can call me Little Joe."

"Where's the sheriff?" I gulp.

"What do you mean?" says Little Joe. "What do you call that silver star on your waistcoat?"

I look down at the sheriff's badge on my chest.

"I'm the sheriff?"

"You crazy, sheriff..." grins the boy.

A woman holding a wailing baby rushes up to me. "Sheriff, these boys are fighting like coyotes," she yells. "It's wrong, I tell you, wrong!" She shoves the baby into my arms and dives into the brawl. "Wait for me!"

Wow! I've landed in this crazy town and I'm the sheriff! OK, I'd better start laying down the law. I sit the baby on the piano and holler:

"Shutuupppppppp!!!"

Everyone stops fighting and looks at me. That was much easier than I thought. My first job as sheriff: bring this rowdy bunch to order. Tick!

I walk through the saloon with my meanest, grittiest face, get to the bar, tip up my hat and say to the barman... "One fizzy lemonade, please!"

"One fizzy lemonade coming up," says the barman. "You want it straight in your hand or shall I slide it down the bar?"

"What do you think?" I reply.

"I'll slide it down the bar," says the barman.

If Adam Virgo could see me now he wouldn't recognize this tough-looking cowboy, with his blood-red neckerchief round his throat and a big brown hat on his head. I'd say, "How ya doing, pardner?" then kick him in the pants and gallop away on my horse.

The barman slides the fizzy lemonade down the bar. I take a long slurp and wipe my mouth with the back of my hand, then let out a really small burp. I hope no one heard me. I do a little "pardon me" under my breath.

I turn round and slowly slide my hand into my pocket.

"He's going for his gun," shouts the blacksmith.

"Don't shoot, mister!" says the barber.

I take my silver dollar and flick it up and down in the palm of my hand, looking really cool.

"You the new sheriff?" says the blacksmith.

"Sure am," I reply. "You got a problem with that?"

"No, no," he mumbles. Then he turns

round and hollers, "Look, boys, we got ourselves another idiot sheriff who thinks he can run the place!"

Everyone rocks around, laughing and whooping. Honestly, I'm supposed to be the sheriff and they're teasing me like I'm just an eight-year-old boy blown into the cowboy world for the very first time. Oh wait, that's exactly what I am...

"If you're a real sheriff, you gotta deal with El Bandido," says a whiskery old man in long johns.

I know that name. El Bandido is the horse thief who pinched Granddad's ass. Everyone in the room starts muttering and shaking their heads. Just one mention of El Bandido has turned them into nervous wrecks.

"If we don't do what El Bandido says," wails the barber, "El Bandido will burn our town to the ground!"

"El Bandido is bad news," says the blacksmith. "Riding round stealing anything El Bandido wants."

"El Bandido even steals piñatas from children's parties," says Little Joe.

"What's a piñata?" I reply.

"You know, those big models made from paper and chicken wire," says the whiskery old man in long johns. "They're filled with candy and hung on string from the ceiling."

"I had a piñata on my last birthday, but El Bandido, he stole my piñata," wails Little Joe.

"I hate him already," I grunt.

Little Joe points to a large poster behind the bar.

"They got a reward out for his capture — twenty-five-thousand dollars! The last sheriff got close, but not close enough!" warns the barber.

"What happened to him?" I ask, trying

not to look nervous.

"Nothing," says the blacksmith, "after he stopped being sheriff, he got a job behind the bar here..."

He turns and points at a skeleton hanging on the wall. "He's our hatstand!"

Everyone roars with laughter.

"Oh dear," I mutter. "He doesn't look too happy."

"You should see his deputy." He spits into a skull-shaped spittoon. "You not yella, are you, sheriff?"

I think "yella" means being a big cowardly custard in cowboy land.

"No man's called me yella before and lived to tell the tale," I reply. This is sort of true. No man has called me yella. Plenty of boys and girls, mind you, and Mrs Bus from the corner shop. "I know how to deal with rough, tough, no-good sorts," I chuckle. "Many a dirty dog I have brought before the law..."

"Like who?" says the whiskery old man.

"Oh, you know..." I try to think of some of the cowboys from the movies. "Billy the Kid, Buffalo Bill ... Wild Bill Hickok. Anyone called Bill or Billy, really."

Everyone round the room starts nodding. I think they're impressed with my answer.

"I like your style, sheriff," says the old man. "You can call me Old Jake, by the way."

"A pleasure to make your acquaintance, Old Jake," I reply.

"Speaking plainly, we're in dire need of your services, sheriff," he continues. "El Bandido and his gang are gonna come and steal our cattle. And if we lose our cattle, what else can we sell at market? We'd be ruined. If we can't trade on our cattle, we'll starve!"

"Sounds like you've got a whole heap of trouble," I reply.

I take a long sip of my lemonade. It's really yummy.

"So here's the thing," continues Old Jake. "We gotta take our cattle to market over in Cactus City and it's real important we keep the whole thing secret from El Bandido! Do you think you can help us, sheriff?"

How can I say no? Saving this little town from El Bandido, that's what sheriffs are for!

I finish the last of my fizzy drink and slam the glass on the table.

"I'm your man!" I announce.

Everyone throws their hats in the air and shoots holes through them. What a waste of hats!

"The lemonade is on the house," says the barman.

"Much obliged, sir," I reply, growing

into my part. "As long as I'm wearing this badge and the office of sheriff counts for something, I will always, ALWAYS, serve the good people of Dungville!"

Everyone cheers. My speech has gone down really well.

"What does this El Bandido look like?" I continue.

"He's got a row of gold teeth," says Old Jake, "and breath like a mule's butt!"

"Eurgh..." I wince.

"Scram, boys," shouts the barman, "we got company..."

Chapter Five

A horse whinnies; a shadow moves across the saloon doors.

The doors fly open.

A stranger in a massive Mexican hat stumbles into the saloon. The barman hides behind the bar, the piano player stops playing and everyone looks around nervously. Why is everybody so scared?

The stranger walks slowly between the tables, chewing a piece of gum.

He leans over the bar and pulls out a jug of liquor.

"Did you see what he just did?" I mumble. "Somebody should call the sheriff."

"You are the sheriff!" whispers Little Joe.

"Oh yes, I forgot," I giggle. "Sorry about that."

The stranger looks at me for a really long time and he chews and he chews and he chews. Then he turns and spits into the spittoon.

"So, you're the new sheriff, yeah..." he says.

"Oh yes," I reply, confidently. "Sheriff by name, sheriff by nature."

I have absolutely no idea what I'm talking about.

"That so, huh?" he replies. "And what is your name, sheriff?"

OK, here we go, I'm going to let him have it – both barrels.

"My name is John Smith," I announce.

There is a bit of a pause before the stranger cracks up laughing.

"Seriously, sheriff," he grunts, "what is your name?"

Oh dear, I just gave it my best shot and he fell about in hysterical hoots. I fix him with my meanest stare as I try to think up a new name for myself. I'd better make this good. After all, they've all got exciting names in the Wild West – Butch this and Sundance that.

"What's the matter, sheriff, can't you speak?" he grins.

"I'm thinking!" I reply.

I carry on thinking for a little bit longer. Everyone leans in, waiting for me to answer. Suddenly, my new name hits me in a blinding moment of genius.

"They call me the Sheriff with No Name!" I growl.

Everyone nods. I think they like the sound of this. It is a very mysterious name.

"That's a very mysterious name," says the stranger. "What's your business here, sheriff?"

"I'm here to protect our cattle from El Bandido," I reply.

"Oooh," says the stranger, "El Bandido! I hear many bad things about this El Bandido – that he is a monster, a villain, an outlaw. I heard he even stole the piñata from a children's birthday party and ate all the candy! And I ask myself: can all this be true?"

The stranger looks round the saloon, drumming his fingers on the bar. "Tell me, where are you taking your cattle? Are you taking them to Cactus City?"

"Yes," I reply. "It's my job to make sure

the cattle don't fall into the hands of El Bandido."

"You don't say," laughs the stranger. "What does he look like, this El Bandido?"

"They say he's got pure gold teeth and his breath smells like a rotten, pongy bottom!"

The stranger suddenly flashes a golden grin.

"You mean it smells like this!" he snarls.

He blows a jet of air in my face. Satan's bum-hole, that stinks!

I stare at the stranger, my eyes popping. "You're El Bandido!"

"Of course," he roars. The stranger throws back his hat. "My horse was bitten in the rear by a rattlesnake," he grunts. "So I sucked out the poison! That is why I have, as you say, breath like a rotten, pongy bottom!"

Wow, he must be one tough cookie, this El Bandido. A whole packet of tough cookies!

"Do you know what my name means in your language?" he growls.

"Uh, the bandit?" I reply.

"OK, so you guessed," he sighs. "But I am still as dangerous as a scorpion in a slipper!"

"We're not scared of you, El Bandido, are we, good people of Dungville?" I cry.

The good people of Dungville have their

heads under the tables and their bottoms in the air.

"Dungville," sneers El Bandido. "The only thing this stinky little town is good for is poop, cowpats, jobbies. Do you know the sound the church bell makes? Dung! Dung! Dung!"

El Bandido cackles for a really long time. When he sees no one else is joining in with his silly joke, he shakes his head. "El Bandido is wasted on you lot!" he shrugs.

Suddenly El Bandido rolls a long leather whip out from under his coat and sends it flicking and cracking across the room. "If you were in my gang, I would soon whip you into shape!" he guffaws.

He slams his glass on the table and does a loud burp. "I would like to thank you for the useful tip about the cattle, Sheriff No-Name," he grins. "My compadres will be waiting for you at our secret hideaway up in the hills."

El Bandido cackles to himself, then dashes out of the saloon with great gusto.

"Are you crazy, sheriff?" says Little Joe. "You just told El Bandido our whole plan. Now he'll be waiting for us. He'll steal our cattle and sell them in the market. And we'll be ruined! RUINED!"

Oh no, I've really goofed this time. Everyone in the saloon stares at me, eyes bulging, mouths wide open.

"Tell us you can protect our cattle, sheriff," says Old Jake.

"Don't worry," I reply. "I'll make sure we get the cattle safely to market. After all, I'm the sheriff and what I say goes!"

Chapter Six

Everyone has gathered in the main street outside the saloon.

"Here you go, sheriff," says Old Jake, leading the herd round the corner, "just make sure you get our cattle safely to Cactus City."

"Don't worry," I smile. "I know what I'm doing!"

I haven't a clue what I'm doing! I wouldn't know Cactus City if it stuck a needle in my bottom. What I need right now is the satnav in Dad's car (even if it was bought on the internet and only speaks Japanese!).

I turn to Little Joe and whisper, "Which way is Cactus City, Little Joe?"

"Oh, it's easy to find Cactus City," says Little Joe. "You see that boulder on the horizon sticking up like a finger?"

Little Joe points to a stone finger sticking high up in the mountains.

"Just aim for that. When you pass the finger, follow the shadow on the ground – it points all the way to Cactus City. Stay on the shadow, you can't go wrong."

"Thanks, Little Joe," I smile, "you're even better than Dad's satnav."

Little Joe looks at me and scratches his head. "I ain't got a clue what you're saying, sheriff," he chortles, "but I like the way you're saying it!"

"You sure you're OK with this?" says the blacksmith.

"Trust me," I grunt in my best cowboy voice, "I'm an old hand at this."

I jump on to my horse and pat her on the neck.

"If you're an old hand at this," says Old Jake, "why are you sitting on a cow?"

I look down and see that my horse has grown a massive pair of udders.

"I was just testing you," I fib.

"Is this your horse, sheriff?" says Little Joe, untying Daisy.

Daisy snorts two blasts of warm air and then does a massive dump on the ground.

"That's my Daisy, all right," I sigh.

"Daisy," cackles Old Jake, "what kind of a name is that?"

Daisy flicks her tail in Old Jake's eye.

"Ouch," hollers Old Jake.

"Don't fail us now, sheriff," says the blacksmith.

"Do I look like I'm about to fail you?" Everyone stares back at me.

I need to prove what an excellent all-round cowboy I am. So I grab some rope and spin it round my head like cowboys are supposed to do. I think they call it lassoing.

The rope slips out of my hand and accidentally lands over an angry bull at the front of the herd. The bull rears up, then charges down the street. Everyone starts clapping and cheering. I lean back in the saddle with my hat held high and shout, "Yeehaw!" That's when I see the rope quickly uncoiling, and just as I work out what is going to happen next, I'm whipped off my feet and dragged along the ground, screaming and hollering, clutching the other end of the rope.

The townsfolk part as the bull pulls me, face down, through the grit and dirt. He thunders round a corner and sends me – still clutching the rope – swinging out wide and on to the back of an old cart. The cart

rolls after the charging bull.

I get to my feet and ride the runaway cart like a chariot.

The bull comes round in a big circle and rages back towards the townsfolk. The excited cheers turn to panic and the townsfolk start to scatter before us, piling into the saloon, diving into the barbershop, shinning up telegraph poles.

Eventually, I yank the rope really hard. The bull digs his heels into the soil, kicking out a gigantic cloud of dust and coming to a sudden stop. The cart slams into the bull's butt and I go flying clean over the top.

The townsfolk look at me, gobsmacked.

"That – was – INCREDIBLE!" gasps Old Jake.

"You sure are a natural," says Little Joe.

"You're going to kick El Bandido's butt," chuckles the blacksmith.

"Good people of Dungville," I declare, "I will deliver your cattle to Cactus City safe and sound."

I jump on to Daisy and cry, "Let's roll 'em out!"

Daisy looks at me, then dawdles along at her own pace. I look back and give the townsfolk of Dungville a great big John Smith thumbs up. This is going to be SO easy.

Wow, it takes a really long time to get the cattle moving. The going is what they call slooooow! I suppose that's fair enough – cattle are a bit big and bulky and when they're not swishing away the flies with their tails, or chewing the grass, they're standing round, barging into each other and, uh ... well, going to the toilet!

It takes a whole hour to move them about

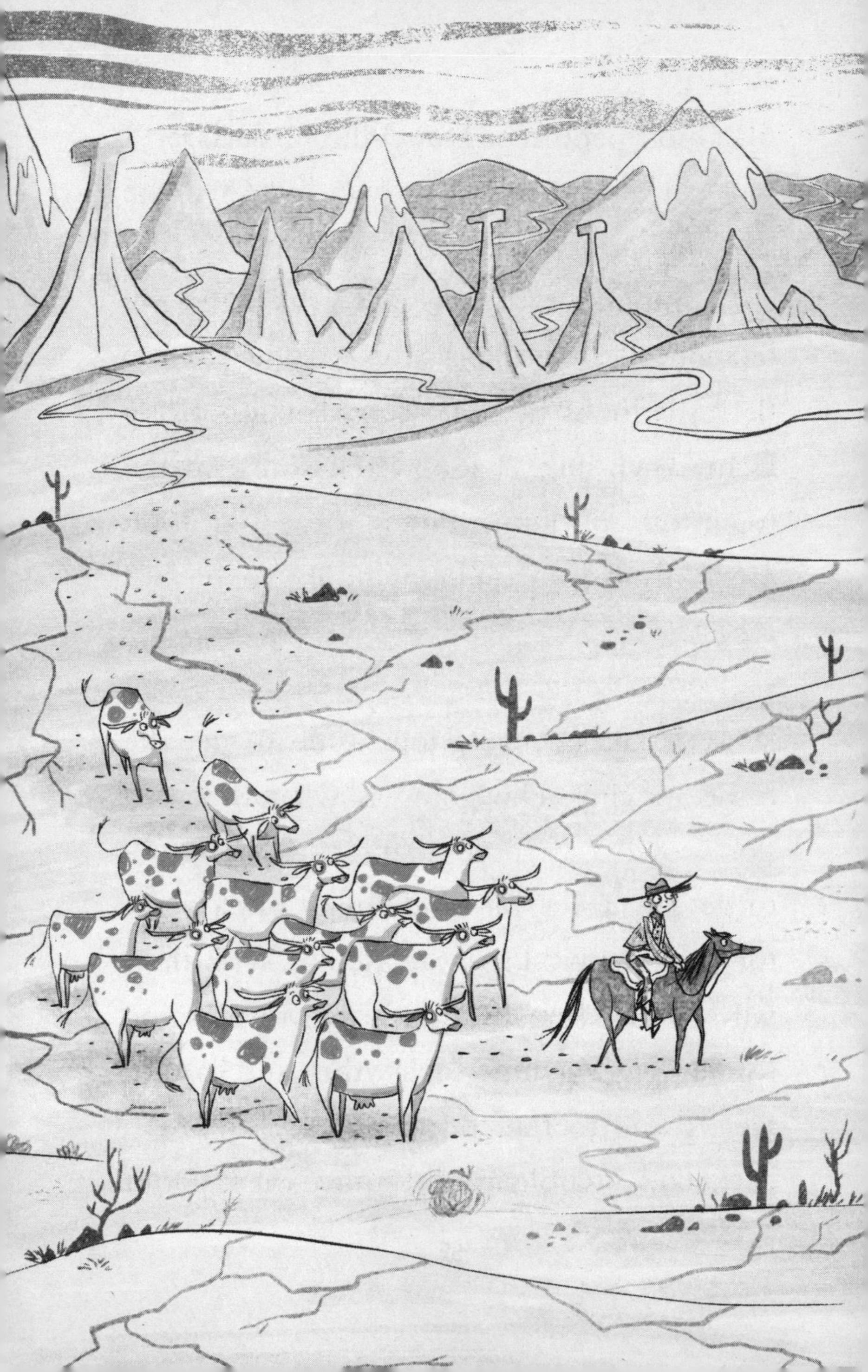

fifty yards. At this rate I'll be in Cactus City next Christmas! I give a few shouts of "yah" and "ha" to get the herd moving a bit faster but it's no good, this lot were born to dawdle. So I sing a song to pass the time. It isn't a very good song, but I've heard Dad sing it round the house when Mum isn't listening. "*Oh take me back home, where the buffalo roam, and you get a house full of poo. . .*"

Eventually we pick up a little pace and leave the desert behind. I drive the cattle over snow-capped peaks, through raging rivers and down craggy slopes. At last I'm starting to get the feel of this cowboy thing. I lean forward and pat Daisy on the neck. "I think we make a pretty good team, Daisy."

Then, suddenly, everything changes. Something goes whizzing past my ear. I look back and see El Bandido and his gang of bandits riding after me with their guns raised and at the ready. Oh dear, oh no, this isn't one of those westerns on the telly where the hero rides off into the sunset, this is real life and – cripes, yikes – those bullets flying round my head are real bullets. To say I'm scared is putting it mildly – I'm pooping baked potatoes!

Another bullet goes whizzing past. This time the cattle get spooked and start to break into a mild jog, which then becomes a firm trot and finally an all-out "look, we're being chased, run for your life" crazy sprint! Who'd have thought these big beasts had it in them, but when they want to run – THEY CAN RUN!

"Come on, Daisy!"

We set off after the cattle, riding up the side of the mountain. I must get to Cactus City before El Bandido! As long as I aim for the big stone finger, I'll be all right.

Hold on, where is the big stone finger? Was it to the left of me? Was it to the right of me? I DON'T KNOW. I can see some other stones but I'm not sure from this angle if any of them are the stone finger Little Joe pointed out to me. One of them looks like a toe, the other one looks like a thumb and the third stone looks more like a massive cucumber.

The big stone finger has COMPLETELY DISAPPEARED. Which way is Cactus City? I'm totally lost. There are no roads and definitely no signposts. In front of me looks just like behind me; left looks like right. The only thing I do know is El Bandido is still chasing me. My heart is thumping, my mouth is dry. My knees would be knocking if they didn't have about half a ton of horse between them. It's time I gave myself a firm talking to.

Steady yourself, you're the sheriff, you've got a

big shiny badge and crazy Daisy the mad mare
and you've got a job to do. So come on, let's get
these cattle to Cactus City!

If I keep riding in a straight line, I'm sure
to hit Cactus City sooner or later.

"Come on, Daisy…"

I drive the cattle on, riding Daisy faster
and faster until we're at full gallop, riding
flat out across the massive desert. But I can't
outrun El Bandido. If horses had rear-view
mirrors I'd catch him in my sights, tearing
across the plain with his band of bandits.

It's time for what they call some hard
riding. I ride like the wind, like MORE than
the wind, like the wind the night after a really
spicy curry! I ride like there's no tomorrow!
Even though tomorrow is Saturday and
there's no school, so it would be nice if there
was a tomorrow. We gallop through scrub
and tumbleweed, cactus plants and bone-dry

desert, past bison skulls and circling vultures. And suddenly, out of nowhere, I see...

The big stone finger! I must have accidentally galloped in a really big circle but at least I'm back on track! All I have to do now is follow the shadow all the way to Cactus City.

I gather the reins and drive the cattle even harder. This is what being a real cowboy is all about. Beating off the bad guys, galloping flat out with the wind in your hair. I drive my cattle up craggy slopes, across raging rivers and along snow-capped peaks until I see, shimmering in the distance, the town I've been trying to find all along.

"Cactus City! That's Cactus City, Daisy! We made it!" I turn back to the tiny dot in the distance that is El Bandido, put my thumb to my nose and blow a huge raspberry.

"Come on, Daisy, let's get these cattle to market!"

Am I the best sheriff ever? I think we all know the answer to that!

Chapter Seven

Cactus City looks just like Dungville.

The barbershop, the blacksmith and the saloon are all identical to Dungville. Then again, you've seen one western you've seen them all, as Dad always says. Even the people look the same. The blacksmith looks just like the blacksmith, the barber looks just like the barber and Little Joe and Old Jake look just like the other Little Joe and Old Jake. And the massive smell of poo is just like

Dungville too. Still, I followed the shadow on the ground so this has to be Cactus City and I must be the greatest sheriff in the land.

Suddenly we hear a loud gunshot. El Bandido rides into town behind me, rifles blazing.

"What are you doing, sheriff?" says Little Joe. "You've led El Bandido right back to Dungville!"

"This can't be Dungville," I laugh. "I followed the shadow. This is Cactus City!"

"It's Dungville," says the barber.

"It's Cactus City!" I reply.

"It's Dungville," shouts El Bandido. "The shadow pointed to Cactus City early in the day, but you got so lost out there, going round in circles, chasing your tail, the sun swung round in the sky so the shadow was pointing back to Dungville! Your sheriff here is an idiot!"

The crowd stare at me. I can feel their disappointment.

El Bandido smiles and shakes his head. "It's time to accept your fate, sheriff," he sighs. "I'm going to steal your cattle and burn your town to the ground."

"I can't let you do that, El Bandido," I cry.

El Bandido looks at me, the smile freezing on his lips, his eyes darkening. "What are you going to do about it, sheriff?" He pulls his whip from his jacket and lets it roll out to the ground. "You're just a nobody!"

Granddad sent me on this adventure to learn to stand up to bullies! Well, John Smith, it's now or never. But how am I going to stop El Bandido pinching the cattle like he once pinched Granddad's ass? Wait a minute ... maybe there is something I can do.

"El Bandido!" I holler. "Nobody calls me nobody!"

I try my best not to look scared, even though my legs are as wobbly as a plate of jelly trifle.

"What are you going to do about it?" snarls El Bandido.

"I'm going to give you ... a cowpat frisbee!"

I grab the flattest, shiniest cowpat off the ground and spin it at El Bandido's head.

The dirty dung bomb explodes in his face. El Bandido rocks on his heels, coughing and spluttering, fanning bits of cow poo away from his head.

"No one gets the better of El Bandido," he rages. "I'm going to teach you a real lesson, sheriff..."

He lifts his whip high in the air and flicks it towards me with a huge CRACK!

"I wouldn't do that, El Bandido," I mutter, backing away nervously.

El Bandido cracks his whip again. "It's a free country, I'll do what I like!" he growls.

He sends the whip's tongue lashing out with another CRACK!

"Seriously," I grunt, "that is not a good idea."

"No one dares tell El Bandido what he can do," he roars.

He rolls out another curl of the whip with a massive CRACK!

"What's the worst that could happen?" he cackles.

"You might cause a ... STAMPEDE!"

The cattle lower their heads and charge down the street, aiming straight for El Bandido.

The bulls scoop El Bandido up and toss him about on their horns. The cows wallop

him with their giant swollen udders. The baby cows kick him in the shins with their hooves.

After trampling El Bandido into the mud, the angry herd turn and bolt out of town, across the desert, towards the mountains in the distance.

Old Jake and Little Joe look at me with open mouths as the herd spread out across the plain and out of sight.

"You've lost us our cattle," sighs Old Jake. "We're ruined!"

The townfolk start coming towards me. Suddenly they don't look so friendly. I might have stopped El Bandido stealing the cattle but that's only because there aren't any cattle to steal. They've bloomin' scarpered! What am I going to do?

"Hold it there!" El Bandido picks himself up off the ground, clutching his trampled whip. "I ain't finished with you, Sheriff No-Name..."

He flicks the whip out, sending the tip wrapping round my wrist.

"Before we settle business," he snarls, "I just wanna know one thing: what's your real name, sheriff?"

Right now I'd love to say the magic words and run away back to my world.

But whilst we're tied together, I might accidentally drag El Bandido back there with me, and then he'd cause all kinds of chaos and mayhem and that would be completely and utterly ... BRILLIANT! This could answer all my problems!

"You wanna know my real name," I announce, "all right, I'll tell you. It's Adam Virgo!"

Bound together by the whip, I take a lungful of dung-filled cowboy air and utter the special magic words to take me home. *"Say it long, say it loud – I'm John Smith and I'm proud!"*

I'm taking El Bandido back with me!

Chapter Eight

El Bandido explodes into Granddad's bedroom, bounces off the end of the bed and splats into the wall. He staggers to his feet, looks around the room, blinking in disbelief, and stutters, "What weird place is this?"

"Welcome to my world!" I holler. "Catch me if you can!"

I fly out of the door and crash into Hayley, accidentally smudging a fresh lick of make-up down the side of her face.

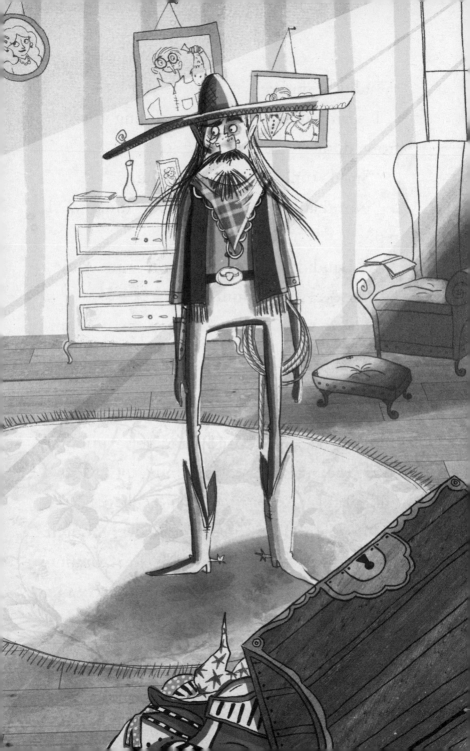

"Idiot!" she yells.

I sprint down the stairs, aiming for the front door.

"Snack-time biccy?" says Mum.

"No thanks, Mum, I'm not hungry," I reply.

El Bandido jumps the stairs and comes eye to eye with Mum.

"Snack-time biccy?" repeats Mum, innocently.

I fly out the front door, down the path and bomb up the street.

I look back and see El Bandido scrambling into the drive, shoving one of Mum's chocolate cookies into his greedy gob.

I'm going to say something I never thought I'd ever say in my entire life: I'm running towards school as fast as my legs will carry me.

"Come back here, you crazy sheriff!" shouts El Bandido.

I sprint across the playing fields, over the road and into the supermarket car park.

"Wheels, wheels, I need wheels. . ." I pant.

I see a shopping trolley at the entrance to the store. It's the perfect escape vehicle.

I jump into the trolley and steer it out of the car park, on to the main road and down the hill towards Cherry Tree School.

"OH NO!!!"

The trolley is chained to a long line of trolleys and stuffed with bags of groceries. I pick up speed, swerving round the mini-roundabout, jumping the humpbacked bridge, charging the traffic lights.

El Bandido sprints down the road, clutching his big Mexican hat to his head.

"You haven't seen the last of El Bandido," he yells.

He throws himself desperately into the last shopping trolley in the trolley train.

Looks like I've got company.

Suddenly, a bottle of ketchup goes whizzing past my head, followed by a bag of potatoes and five fat pork sausages. I see El Bandido in the last trolley, loading his fists with grocery missiles. Time to fight back.

I gather everything up and return fire.

"Bangers and mash with extra tomato sauce – my favourite!" I chortle.

"I'm coming to get you, Adam Virgo!" screams El Bandido.

El Bandido leapfrogs into the next trolley in the line. This is like one of those cowboy chases over train carriage roofs, but in shopping trolleys!

"You will regret the day you messed with me," he snarls.

I steer the trolley round a sharp corner towards the school. The rest of the trolley train swings out wildly behind it.

"You don't get rid of me that easily, sheriff!" screams El Bandido as he jumps into the trolley behind my trolley.

I look up and see a huge rubbish truck blocking the road, its jaws opened wide to show a massive mound of rubbish inside. Unless I take immediate action, this is going to end ugly.

"Just one more trolley," says El Bandido, "and I have you!"

"I wouldn't be so sure about that, El Bandido..." I cry. I fiddle around inside my pocket and pull out the lucky silver dollar Granddad gave me. I've been waiting for my chance to use this.

I slot the silver dollar into the lock and tug my trolley free of the rest of the trolleys.

"See you around, El Bandido," I smile.

I steer the trolley down the side of the rubbish truck towards Cherry Tree. El Bandido and the shopping trolley fly into

the back of the rubbish truck.
The jaws close around him
with one satisfying
gulp.

Chapter Nine

I skid through the school gates, crash land the trolley on a grassy bank and sprint towards the playing field. School sports day, here I come!

Adam Virgo waits for me, dressed in a full-on American football strip. We've all had to borrow our strips for school sports day but Adam Virgo gets his own strip with his name written on the back because as far as Mr and Mrs Virgo are concerned, what little angel Adam wants – little angel Adam gets.

"Well, well, it's Mr Nobody!" laughs Virgo. "Prepare to be pulped, John Smith!"

He tightens his throat strap and trots on to the field.

I run across the playground, round the back of the school canteen and into the changing room. Rows of American football strips hang neatly on pegs. I pull on a strip, tug the helmet firmly over my head, pull down the visor and jog confidently out towards the field of play.

Just as I take to the pitch, I see El Bandido stumbling through the school gates.

The referee blows the whistle and we start to play a game of American football.

Adam Virgo picks up the ball and runs down the field, ducking and dodging the tackles, skipping past all the other players, effortlessly pushing aside the opposition.

He's about to do a spectacular touchdown when he's felled by an old-style bandit from

the Wild West with a big
sombrero hat, a chest criss-
crossed with bullets and
smelling of sour milk and
babies' nappies.

El Bandido
picks Adam

Virgo up and spins him round.

"I see the name on the back of your shirt," says El Bandido. "You are Adam Virgo, yes?"

Adam Virgo nods underneath his helmet.

"I have you now, Adam Virgo," laughs El Bandido, "and I will have my revenge!"

El Bandido starts to kick Adam Virgo in the pants all around the school playing field.

Everyone falls around laughing.

"Get off, stop it!" yelps Virgo.

He runs out of the school gates with El Bandido just behind, planting his pointy cowboy boots in the heart of Adam Virgo's butt.

After that, Adam Virgo pretty much left me alone, especially after I magicked El Bandido back into the arms of Old Jake and Little

Joe so they could claim their reward and
buy a new herd of cattle.

My adventure in the Wild West was

definitely worth it. I helped save Dungville, beat the bad guys and best of all I learnt how to stand up to my very own home-grown bully. I say a massive "Yeeeeeeee-haaaaaaaaw" to that!

But do you think anybody will believe me when I tell them I really was a cowboy in the old Wild West? Of course they won't, because I'm John Smith.

But you know, don't you…

Have you read John Smith's other

NOT BORING!

adventures?

John Smith is NOT BORING!

SPACEMAN John THE (NEARLY) BOLD

by Johnny Smith

I settle into my seat, buckle my belt, power up my spaceship and head for home. Goodbye, little satellite. Goodbye, space. I'm going to watch United win the final.

The rockets roar as I turn the spaceship in a big circle and steer her towards Earth.

I might be on the far side of the Milky Way but an empty tummy is an empty tummy. Time I found myself a little space snack.

I ping the glove box open and search around for another travel sweet. "Oh dear. . ."

The box is completely empty.

I unbuckle my belt and float off looking for a nibble. As I drift to the back of the spaceship, I see a big cupboard.

Space Food, reads the sign on the door. "What have we got in here?"

I've heard all about space food — bite-sized morsels that taste like entire meals. Burger and chips! Sticky toffee pudding! Cheese toasties! The mind boggles!

Inside the cupboard are lots of little cardboard cartons in neat rows. I pull a carton off the shelf.

"Chicken chow mein. . ."

I flip the special space carton over and read off the back.

"Oodles of noodles in a finger-licking chicken sauce."

Scrum-diddly-umptious!

"Heat in special space cooker for six minutes. Check product is piping hot before serving."

I whack the space food in the space cooker until it makes a little ding. It tastes just like the ready meals Mum brings home from the supermarket. I close my eyes and savour the delicious tastes.

"Mmmmmmmm..."

When I open my eyes, I am face-to-face with another spaceman, staring right back at me!

The spaceman lunges at me, making a horrible growl. Underneath his helmet I see big bulging eyes and a nasty, drooling mouth.

"AAAAARRRRGGGHHHH!!!"

I push away and go spinning head over heels, crashing into the flight control panel, accidentally nudging the turbo-thrust-thingy with my bottom.

The boosters flare up; the rockets spit fire into space. The spaceship kicks on at a million miles a second. The lights start flashing on the flight control panel, the alarm starts beeping. The furry dice are flying about like crazy.

"Mission control, mission control, do you read me?" I scream. Then I remember, mission control is sitting on the loo reading a copy of the *Racing Times*.

Suddenly the darkness of space is lit up with flashes of bright white light. Out of the window I see we're heading for a comet!!!

I dive for the steering wheel and turn the spaceship sideways. As I do, the spaceman does a somersault and crashes into me.

"Get off me! Get off me!" I gasp.

We strike the tail of the comet.

The spaceship goes spinning round in circles. Lumps of comet smash into the side of the spaceship; fire scorches the nose. Ice

peppers the windscreen. I try pressing the windscreen wipers but they jam. Outside, red-hot flames lick at the window.

"Mission control, mission control, do you copy?" I holler, desperately.

The radio crackles into life.

"Everyman One, this is mission control, sorry about that. I just nipped off for a rich tea biscuit and I thought whilst I was in that part of the world I might like to make myself a nice cup of tea..."

"Mission control, we have a problem!"

"So anyway, I made myself a cup of tea, and do you know what? I couldn't find the sugar..."

"Mission control, we have a problem!" I repeat.

"So I had to borrow a spoon of sugar from whatshername next door..." says mission control. "You know, her with the leg..."

"MISSION CONTROL!!!"

"Anyway, how can I be of service?"

"There's another spaceman in the spaceship!" I scream.

"Don't be daft, Spaceman John," says mission control. "This is a one-man flight."

"Oh no!" I shriek.

The spaceship is hurtling towards a massive, lifeless rock.

"I think we're going to crash, Granddad," I cry.

"You're breaking up on me," says mission control. "Say that again..."

"Crash positions!"

The spaceship slams into the rock.

The hatch explodes and we both fall out at a zillion miles an hour. We tumble across the craters, wrapped up in each other's arms and legs, one big spacemen bundle, with the spaceship skidding just behind us.

Eventually we roll to a stop.

I scramble to my feet and holler at the other spaceman.

"You made me crash my spaceship..."

The spaceman takes a step towards me. This is the most scared I've been since I slept head to toe with Hayley in the same bed.

I peer into the helmet and see the face on the inside in all its amazing detail. It is a face that turns my heart ice cold with fear.

Other
NOT BORING!
adventures from
John Smith

Johnny Smith is an experienced animation and live-action screenwriter. As one half of Sprackling and Smith, the comedy screenwriting team, he sold numerous original feature film scripts here and in Hollywood, including Disney's box office hit GNOMEO & JULIET. He lives in London with his wife and children.